W9-CIQ-448

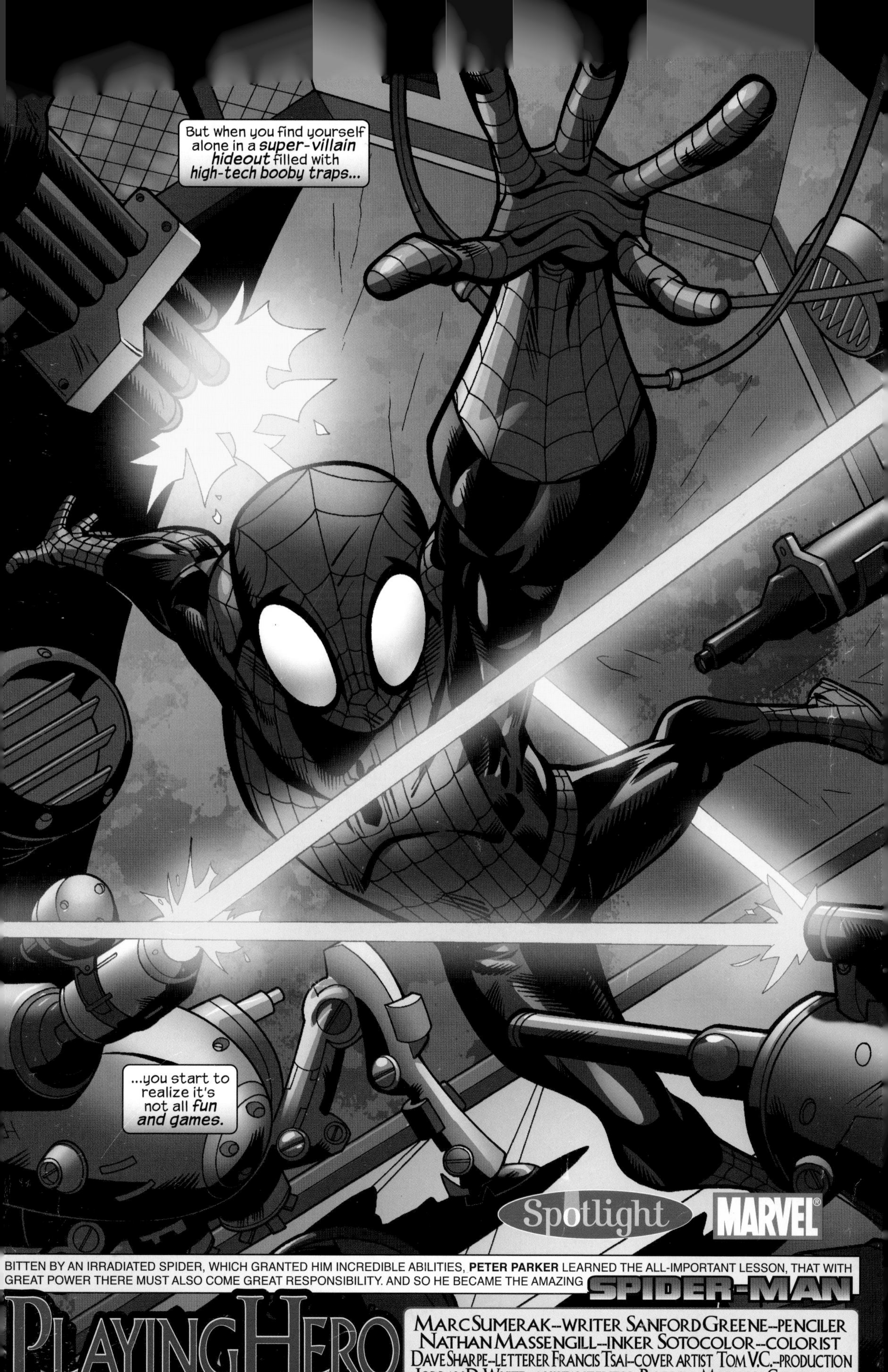
But when you find yourself alone in a *super-villain hideout* filled with *high-tech booby traps...*
...you start to realize it's not all *fun and games.*
Spotlight
MARVEL

BITTEN BY AN IRRADIATED SPIDER, WHICH GRANTED HIM INCREDIBLE ABILITIES, **PETER PARKER** LEARNED THE ALL-IMPORTANT LESSON, THAT WITH GREAT POWER THERE MUST ALSO COME GREAT RESPONSIBILITY. AND SO HE BECAME THE AMAZING **SPIDER-MAN**

PLAYING HERO

MARC SUMERAK--WRITER SANFORD GREENE--PENCILER
NATHAN MASSENGILL--INKER SOTOCOLOR--COLORIST
DAVE SHARPE--LETTERER FRANCIS TSAI--COVER ARTIST TOM V.C.--PRODUCTION
JORDAN D. WHITE--ASSISTANT EDITOR PANICCIA, MACCHIO--CONSULTING
NATHAN COSBY--EDITOR JOE QUESADA--EDITOR IN CHIEF DAN BUCKLEY--PUBLISHER

VISIT US AT
www.abdopublishing.com

Reinforced library bound edition published in 2011 by Spotlight, a division of the ABDO Group, 8000 West 78th Street, Edina, Minnesota 55439. Spotlight produces high-quality reinforced library bound editions for schools and libraries. Published by agreement with Marvel Characters, Inc.

Printed in the United States of America, Melrose Park, Illinois.
042010
092010
This book contains at least 10% recycled material.

Library of Congress Cataloging-in-Publication Data

Sumerak, Marc.
  Playing hero / story, Marc Sumerak ; art, Sanford Greene. -- Reinforced library ed.
     p. cm. -- (Spider-Man (Series))
  "Marvel."
  Summary: Spider-Man must team up with a bullying braggart to defeat a video game that has come to life.
  ISBN 978-1-59961-778-7
  1. Graphic novels. [1. Graphic novels. 2. Superheroes--Fiction. 3. Video games--Fiction. 4. Pride and vanity--Fiction.] I. Greene, Sanford, ill. II. Title.
  PZ7.7.S86Pl 2010
  741.5'973--dc22
                    2009052842

All Spotlight books have reinforced library bindings and are manufactured in the United States of America.

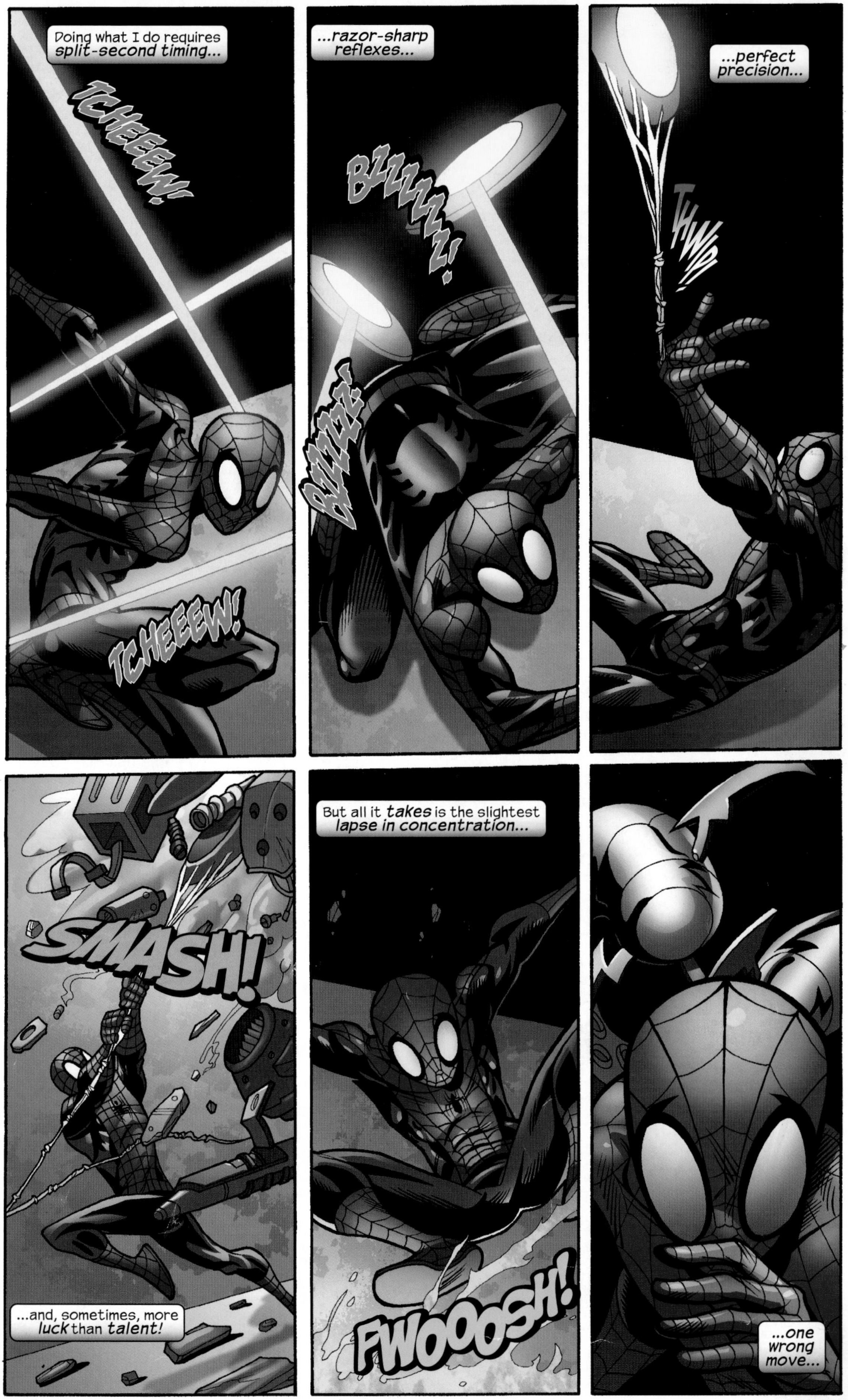
Doing what I do requires split-second timing...
TCHEEEW!
TCHEEEW!
...razor-sharp reflexes...
BZZZZZZZ!
BZZZZZ!
...perfect precision...
THWIP!
SMASH!
...and, sometimes, more luck than talent!
But all it takes is the slightest lapse in concentration...
FWOOOSH!
...one wrong move...

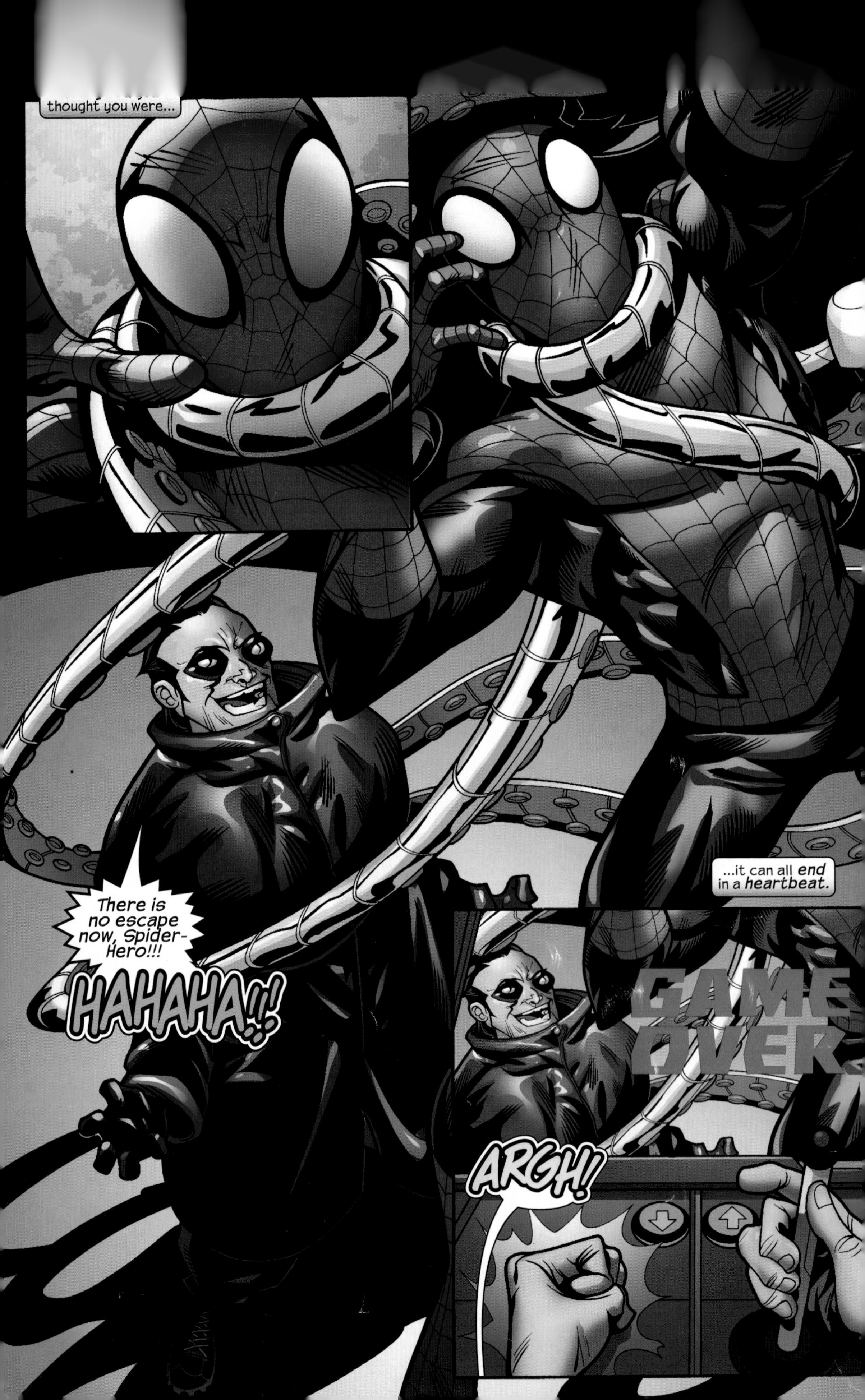

thought you were...
...it can all end in a heartbeat.
There is no escape now, Spider-Hero!!!
HAHAHA!!!
GAME OVER
ARGH!

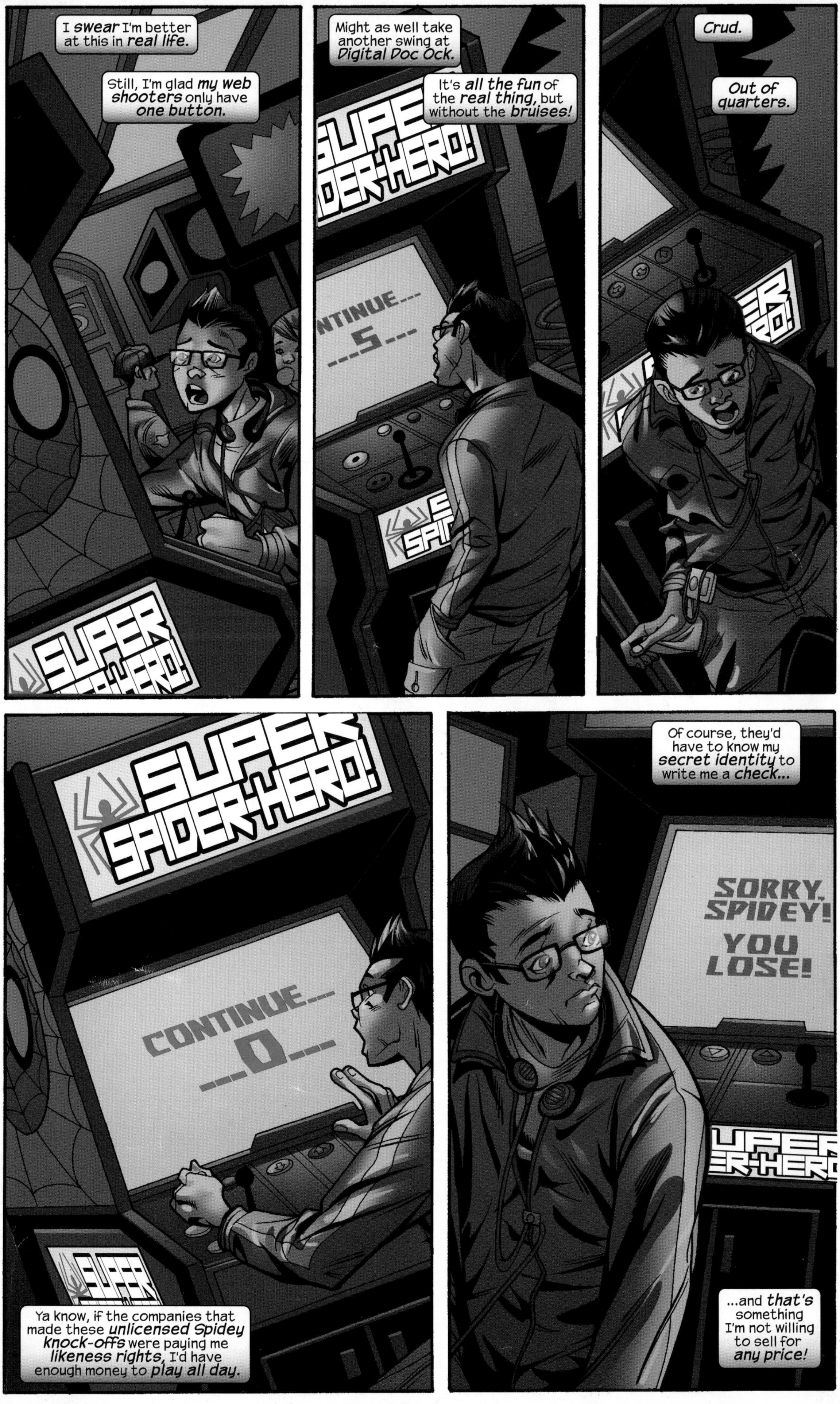
I swear I'm better at this in real life.
Still, I'm glad my web shooters only have one button.
SUPER SPIDER-HERO!
Might as well take another swing at Digital Doc Ock.
It's all the fun of the real thing, but without the bruises!
CONTINUE... 5...
Crud.
Out of quarters.
SUPER SPIDER-HERO!
CONTINUE... 0...
Ya know, if the companies that made these unlicensed Spidey knock-offs were paying me likeness rights, I'd have enough money to play all day.
Of course, they'd have to know my secret identity to write me a check...
SORRY, SPIDEY! YOU LOSE!
...and that's something I'm not willing to sell for any price!

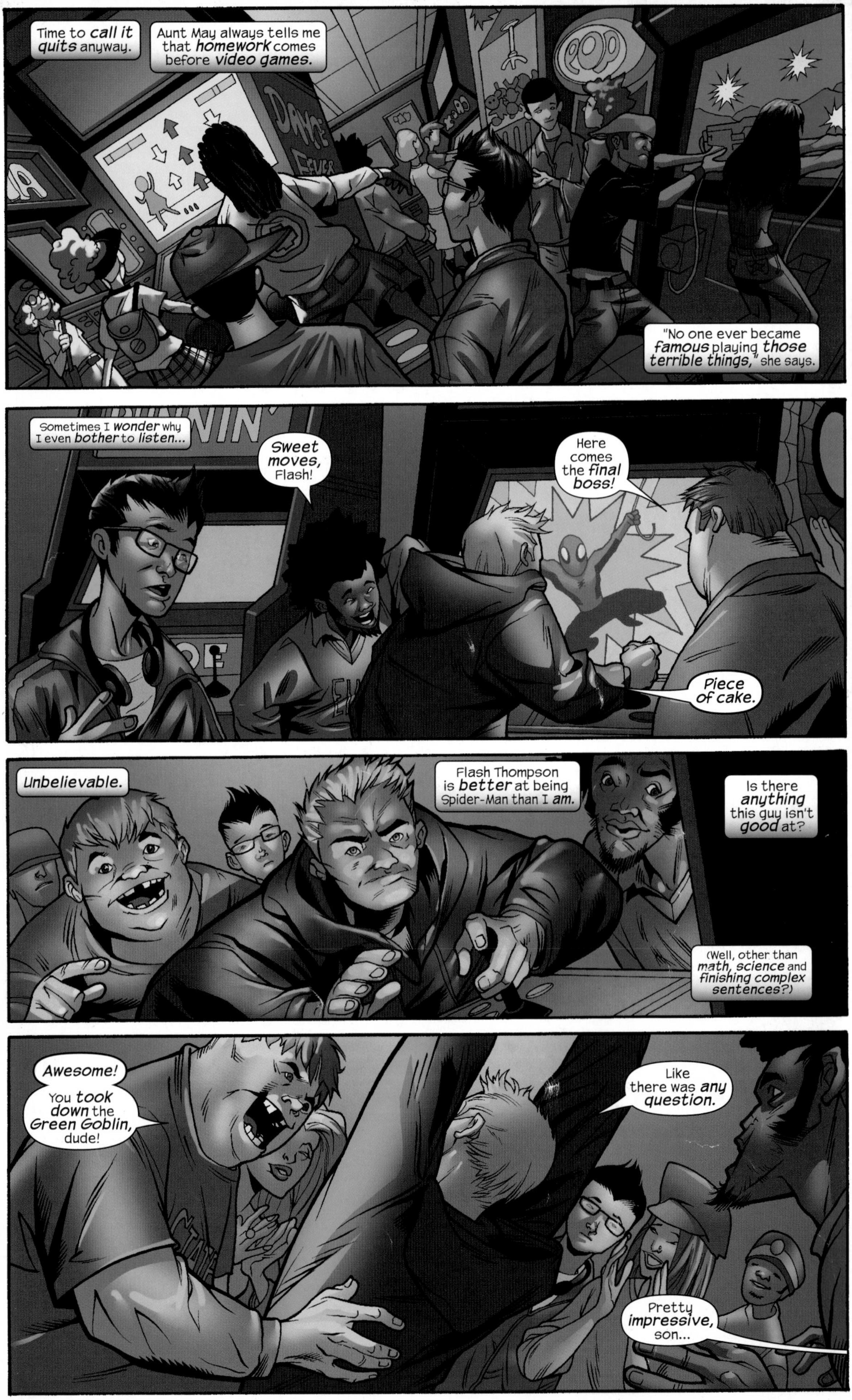

Time to call it quits anyway.
Aunt May always tells me that homework comes before video games.
"No one ever became famous playing those terrible things," she says.
Sometimes I wonder why I even bother to listen...
Sweet moves, Flash!
Here comes the final boss!
Piece of cake.
Unbelievable.
Flash Thompson is better at being Spider-Man than I am.
Is there anything this guy isn't good at?
(Well, other than math, science and finishing complex sentences?)
Awesome!
You took down the Green Goblin, dude!
Like there was any question.
Pretty impressive, son...

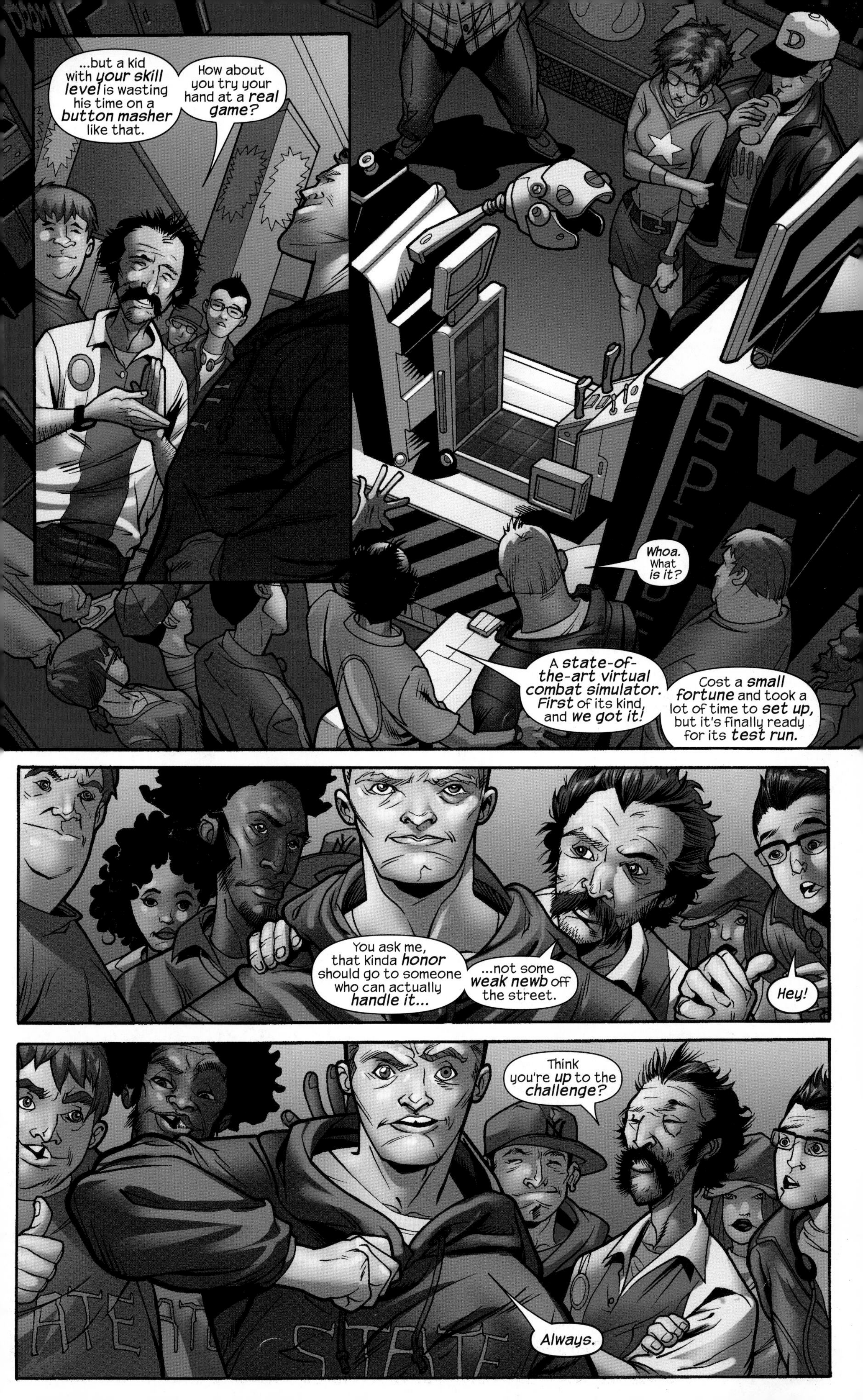
...but a kid with your skill level is wasting his time on a button masher like that.
How about you try your hand at a real game?
Whoa. What is it?
A state-of-the-art virtual combat simulator. First of its kind, and we got it!
Cost a small fortune and took a lot of time to set up, but it's finally ready for its test run.
You ask me, that kinda honor should go to someone who can actually handle it...
...not some weak newb off the street.
Hey!
Think you're up to the challenge?
Always.

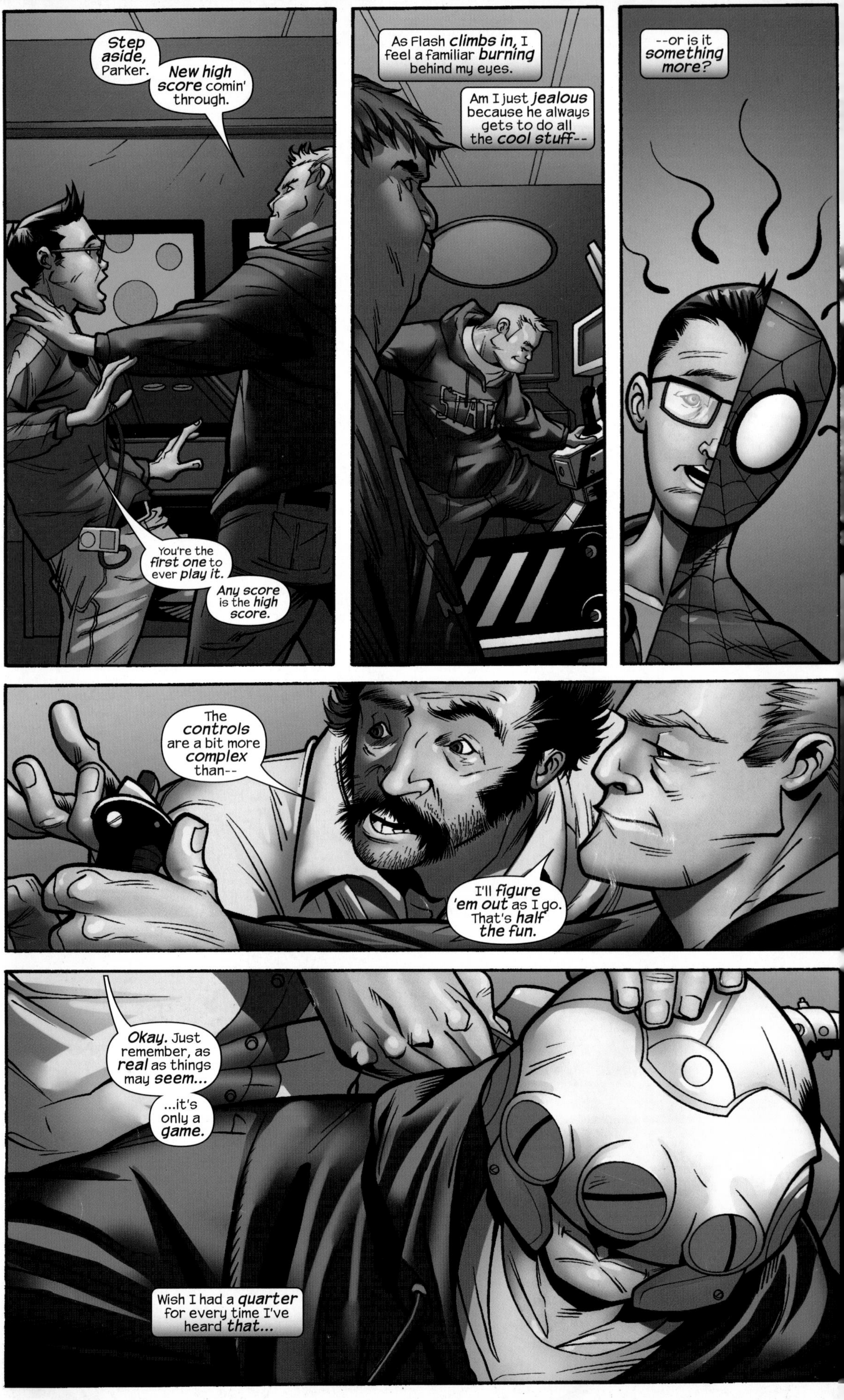
Step aside, Parker.
New high score comin' through.
You're the first one to ever play it.
Any score is the high score.
As Flash climbs in, I feel a familiar burning behind my eyes.
Am I just jealous because he always gets to do all the cool stuff--
--or is it something more?
The controls are a bit more complex than--
I'll figure 'em out as I go. That's half the fun.
Okay. Just remember, as real as things may seem...
...it's only a game.
Wish I had a quarter for every time I've heard that...

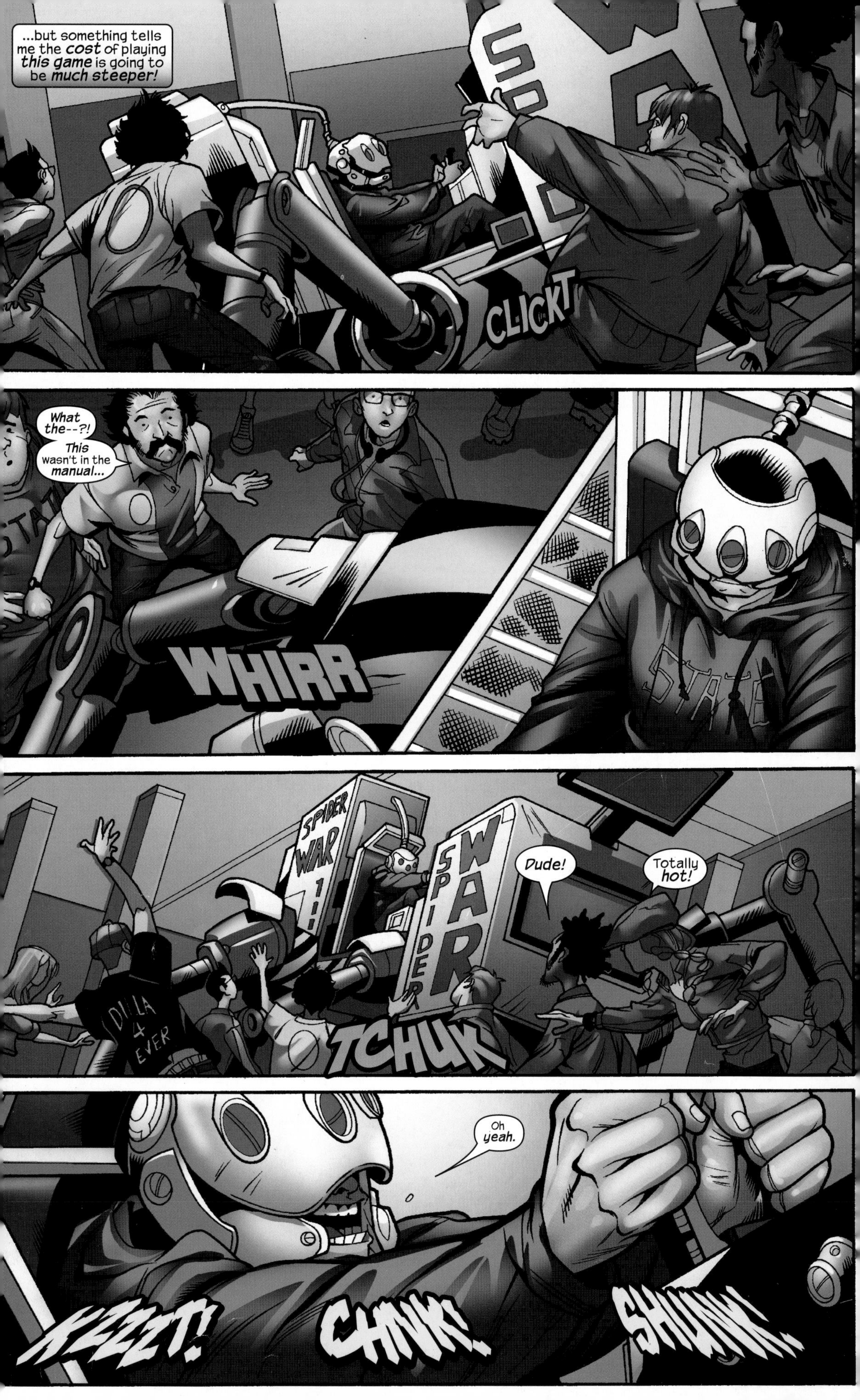

...but something tells me the *cost* of playing *this game* is going to be *much steeper!*
CLICKT
What the--?! This wasn't in the *manual*...
WHIRR
SPIDER WAR 1
SPIDER WAR
Dude!
Totally *hot!*
DILLA 4 EVER
TCHUK
Oh yeah.

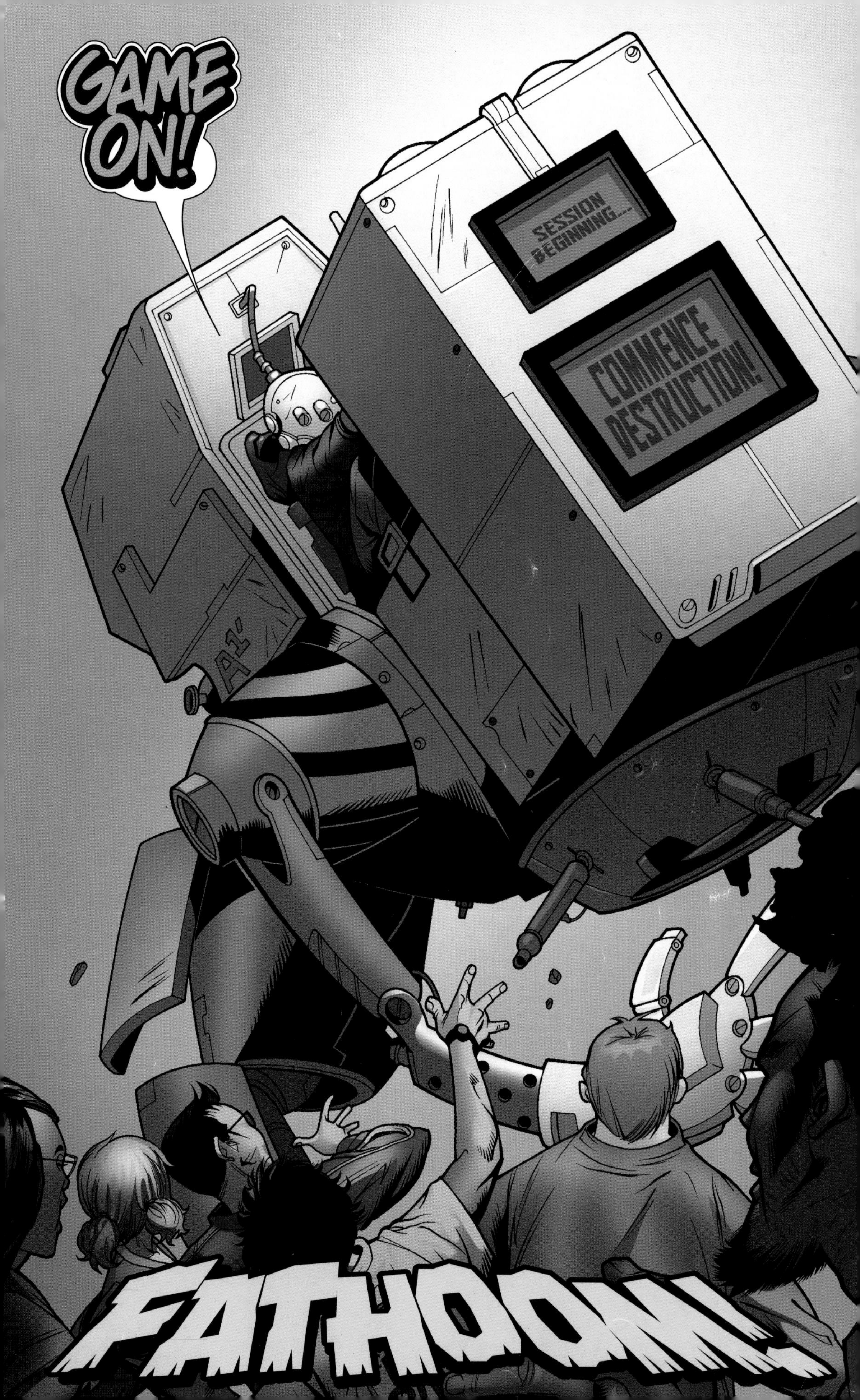
GAME ON!
SESSION BEGINNING...
COMMENCE DESTRUCTION!
FATHOOM!

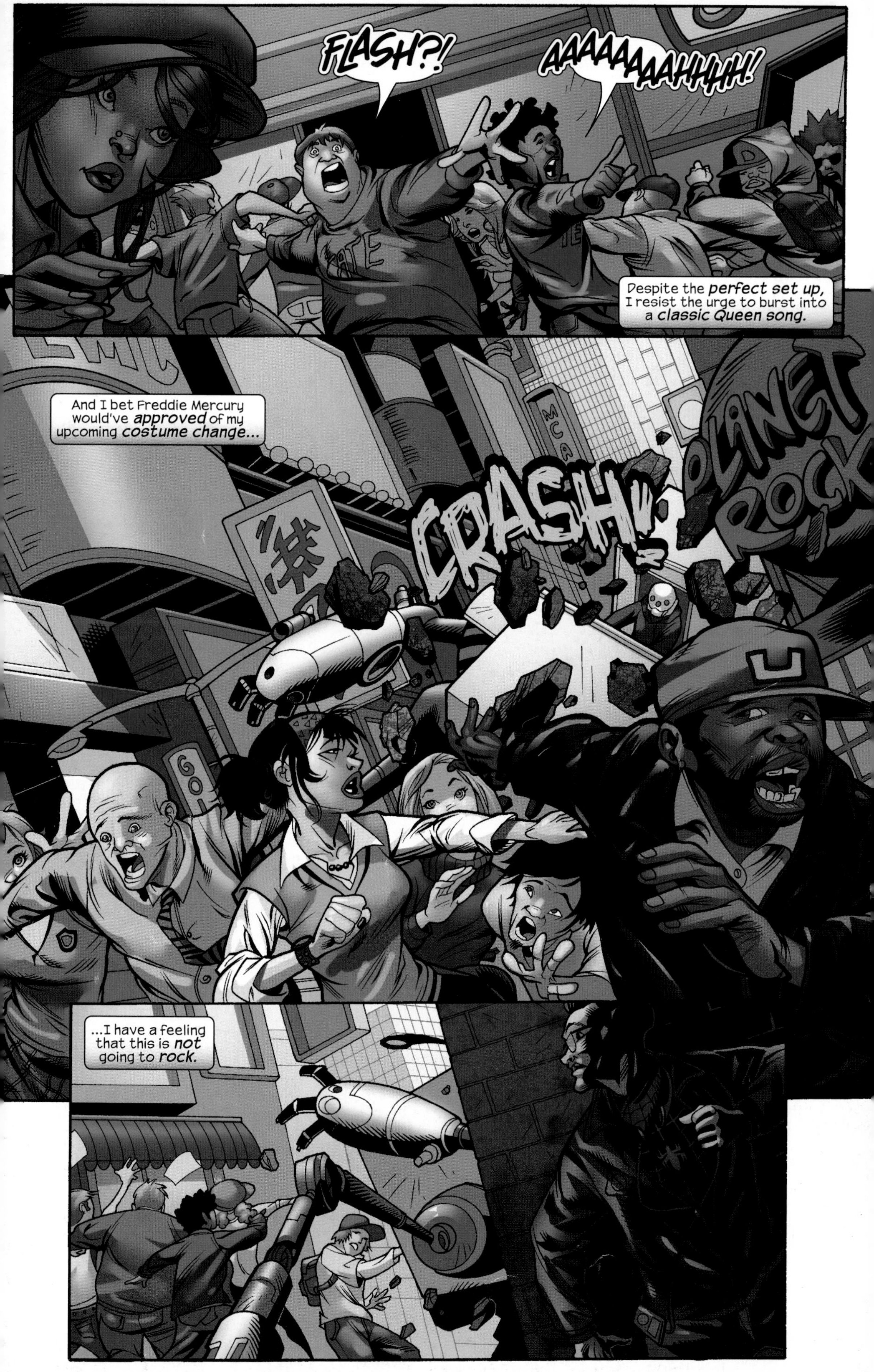
FLASH?!
AAAAAAAAHHHH!
Despite the perfect set up, I resist the urge to burst into a classic Queen song.
And I bet Freddie Mercury would've approved of my upcoming costume change...
CRASH!
PLANET ROCK
...I have a feeling that this is not going to rock.

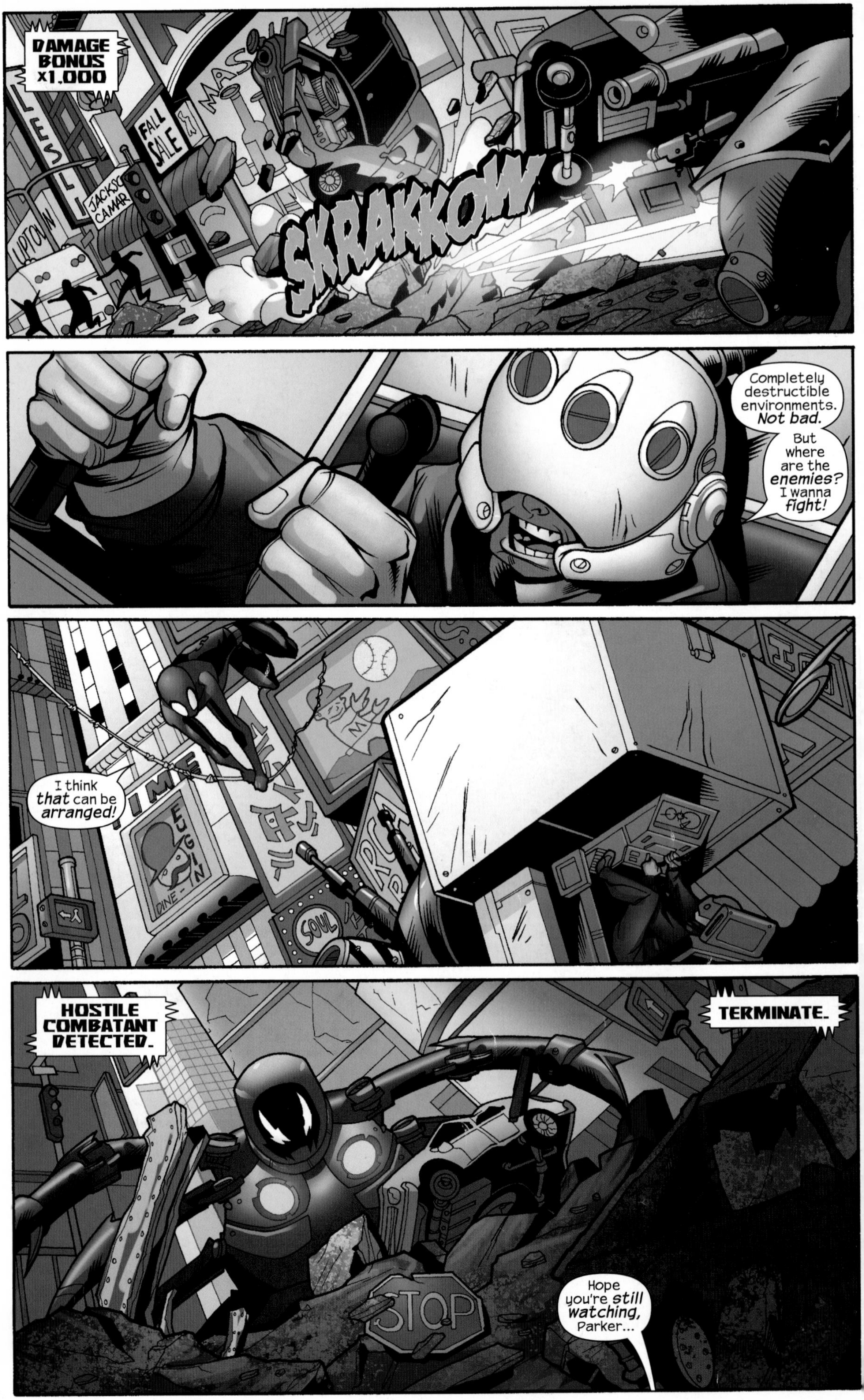
DAMAGE BONUS x1,000
SKRAKKOW
FALL SALE
UPTOWN
JACKSO CAMAR
Completely destructible environments. Not bad.
But where are the enemies? I wanna fight!
I think that can be arranged!
DINE
SOUL
HOSTILE COMBATANT DETECTED.
TERMINATE.
STOP
Hope you're still watching, Parker...

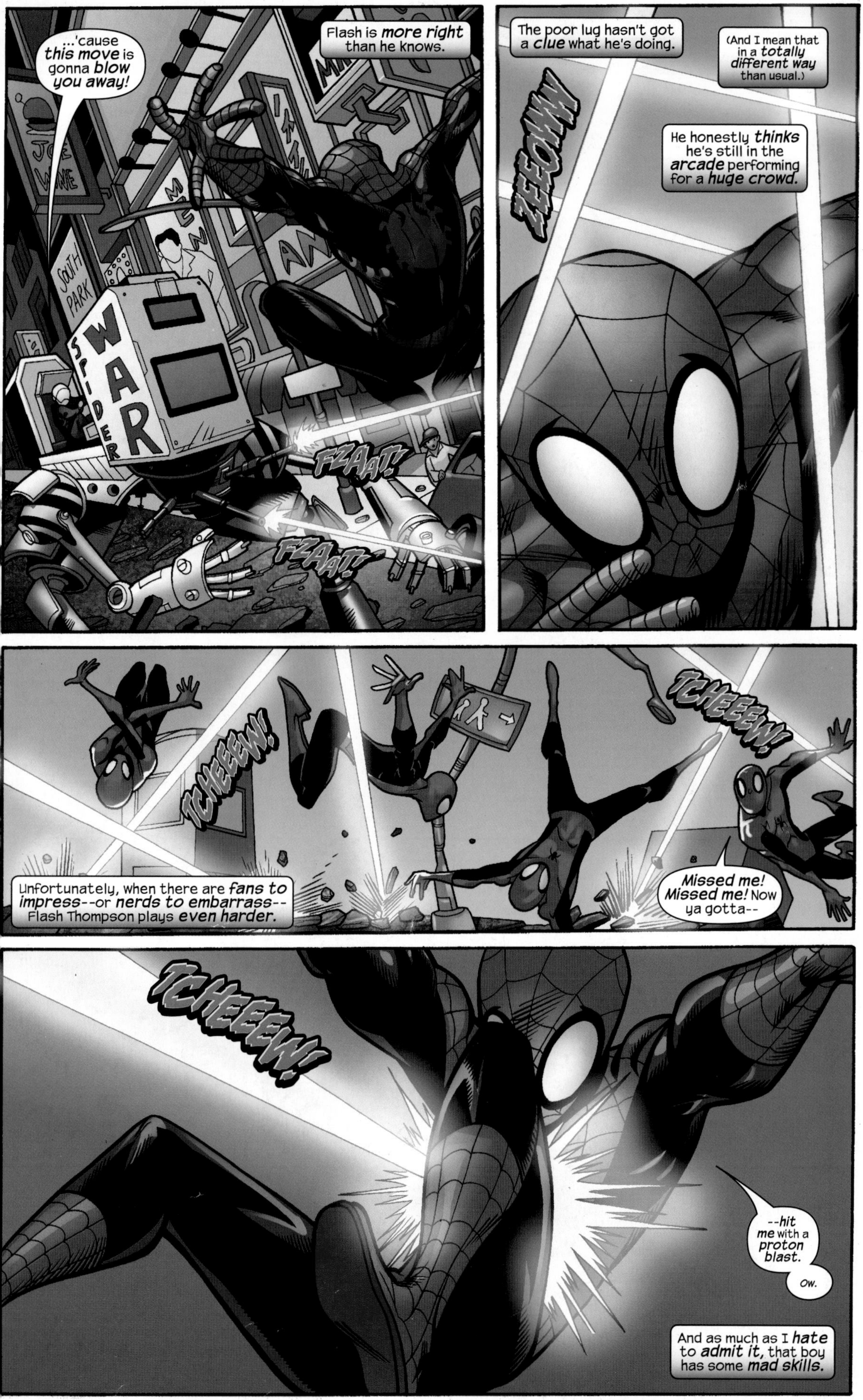

...'cause this move is gonna blow you away!
Flash is more right than he knows.
FZAAT!
FZAAT!
The poor lug hasn't got a clue what he's doing.
(And I mean that in a totally different way than usual.)
ZEEOWW
He honestly thinks he's still in the arcade performing for a huge crowd.
TCHEEEEW!
TCHEEEEW!
Unfortunately, when there are fans to impress--or nerds to embarrass--Flash Thompson plays even harder.
Missed me! Missed me! Now ya gotta--
TCHEEEEW!
--hit me with a proton blast.
Ow.
And as much as I hate to admit it, that boy has some mad skills.

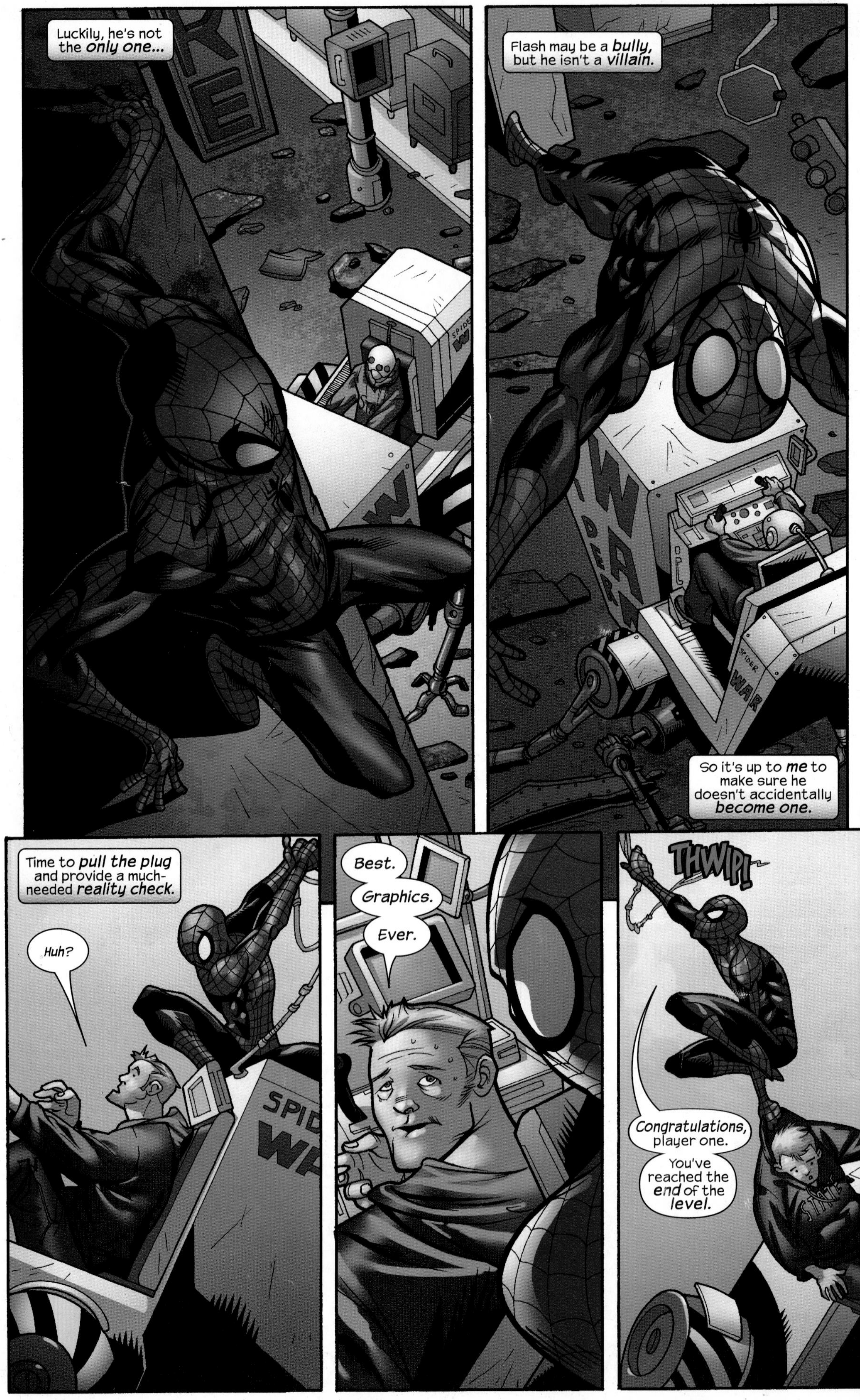
Luckily, he's not the *only one*...
Flash may be a *bully*, but he isn't a *villain*.
So it's up to *me* to make sure he doesn't accidentally *become one*.
Time to *pull the plug* and provide a much-needed *reality check*.
Huh?
Best.
Graphics.
Ever.
THWIP!
Congratulations, player one.
You've reached the *end* of the *level*.

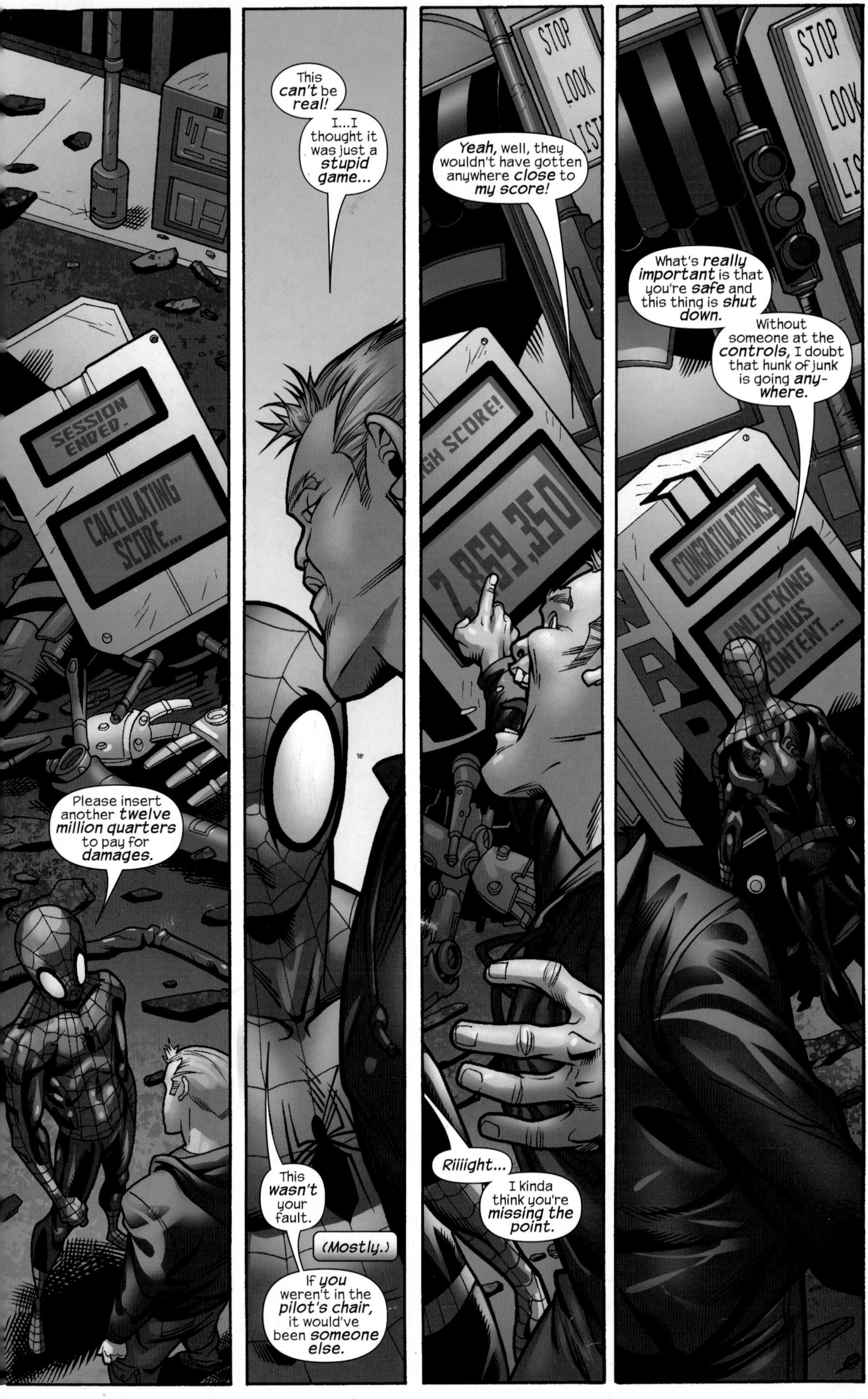
SESSION ENDED.
CALCULATING SCORE...
Please insert another twelve million quarters to pay for damages.
This can't be real!
I...I thought it was just a stupid game...
This wasn't your fault.
(Mostly.)
If you weren't in the pilot's chair, it would've been someone else.
STOP LOOK
Yeah, well, they wouldn't have gotten anywhere close to my score!
GH SCORE!
2,869,350
Riiiight...
I kinda think you're missing the point.
STOP LOOK
What's really important is that you're safe and this thing is shut down.
Without someone at the controls, I doubt that hunk of junk is going any-where.
CONGRATULATIONS!
UNLOCKING BONUS CONTENT...

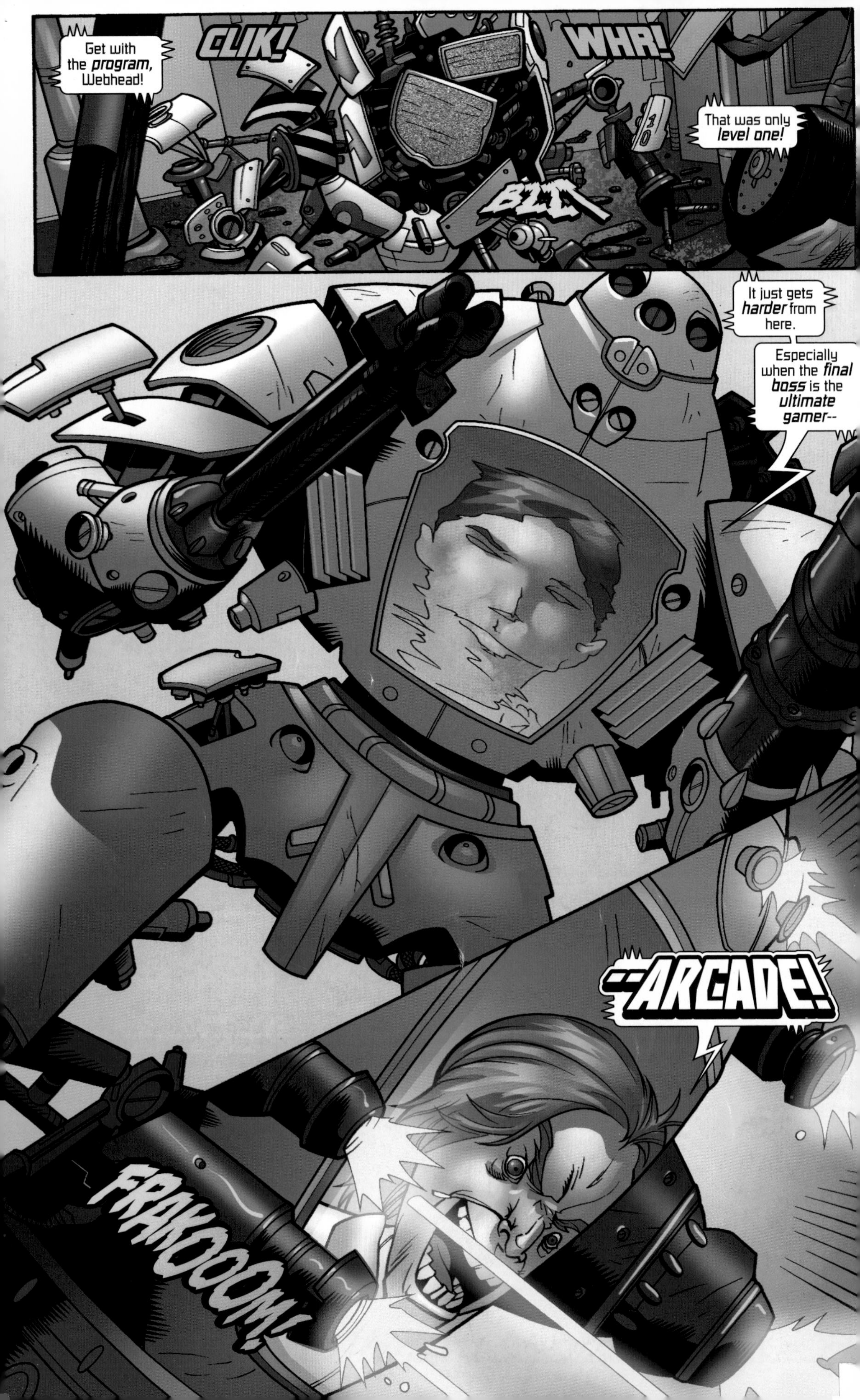
Get with the program, Webhead!
CLIK!
WHR!
That was only level one!
BZZT
It just gets harder from here.
Especially when the final boss is the ultimate gamer--
--ARCADE!
FRAKOOOOM!

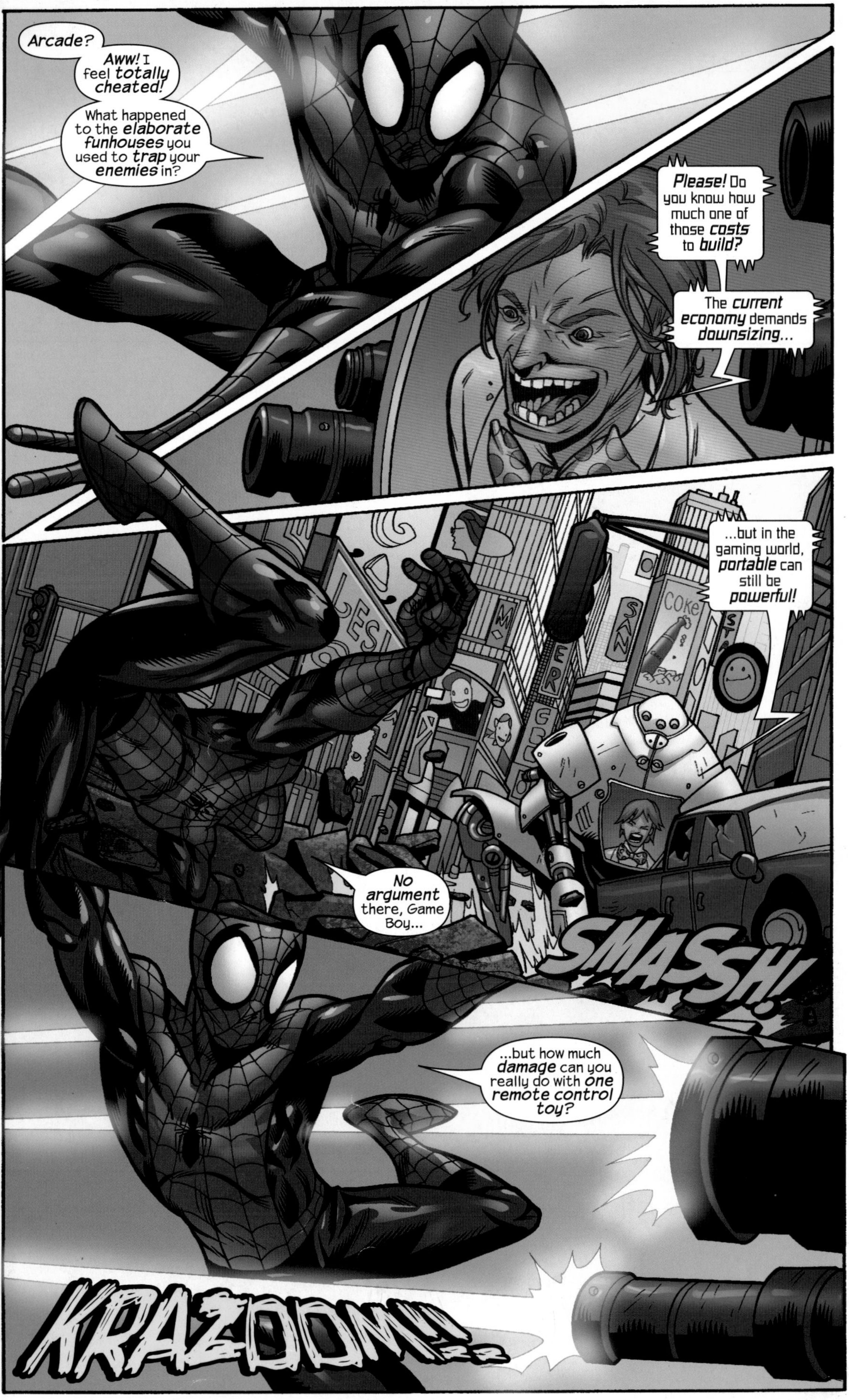

Arcade?
Aww! I feel totally cheated!
What happened to the elaborate funhouses you used to trap your enemies in?
Please! Do you know how much one of those costs to build?
The current economy demands downsizing...
...but in the gaming world, portable can still be powerful!
No argument there, Game Boy...
SMASSH!
...but how much damage can you really do with one remote control toy?
KRAZOOM!!

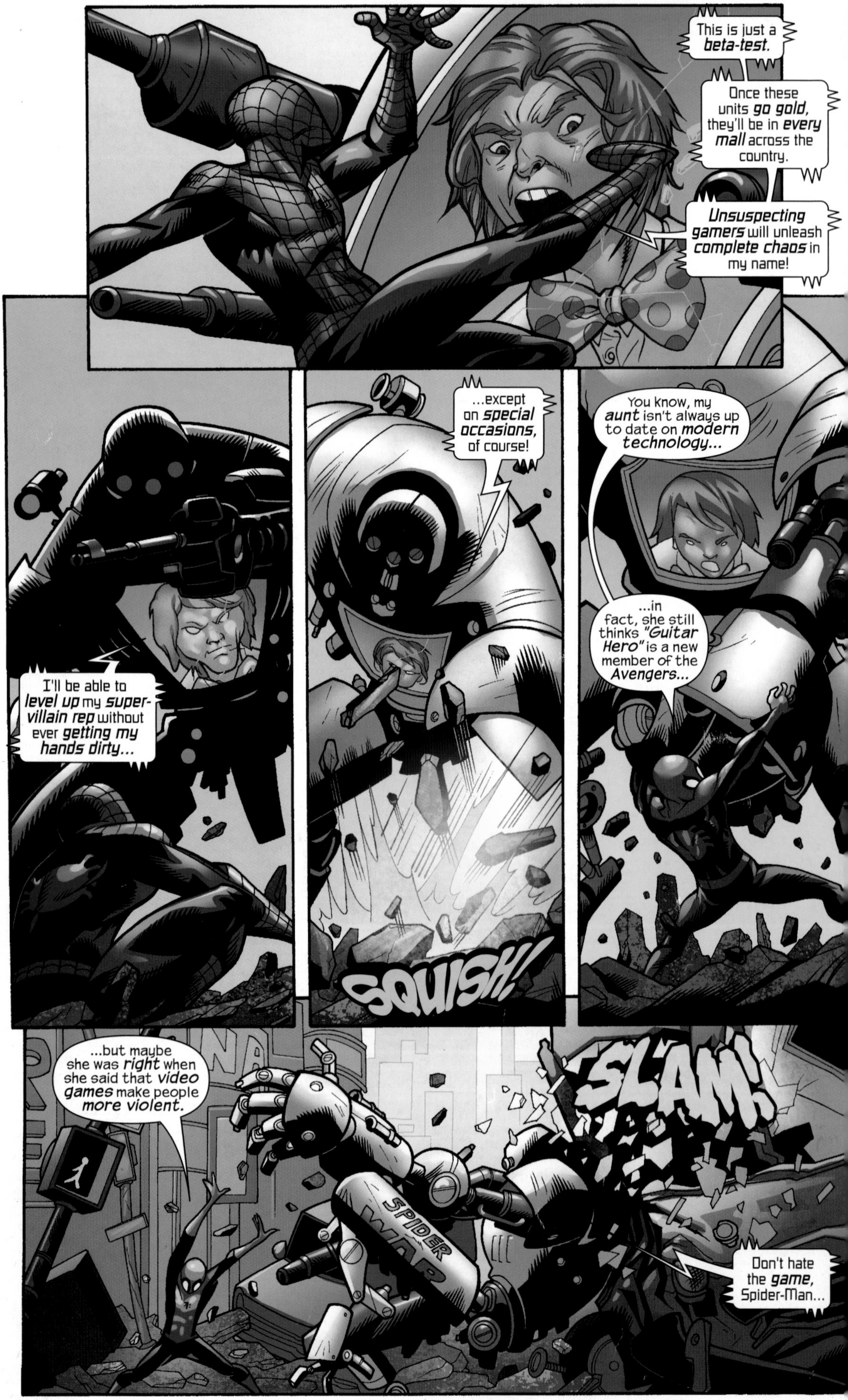
This is just a beta-test.
Once these units go gold, they'll be in every mall across the country.
Unsuspecting gamers will unleash complete chaos in my name!
I'll be able to level up my super-villain rep without ever getting my hands dirty...
...except on special occasions, of course!
SQUISH!
You know, my aunt isn't always up to date on modern technology...
...in fact, she still thinks "Guitar Hero" is a new member of the Avengers...
...but maybe she was right when she said that video games make people more violent.
SLAM!
SPIDER WAR
Don't hate the game, Spider-Man...

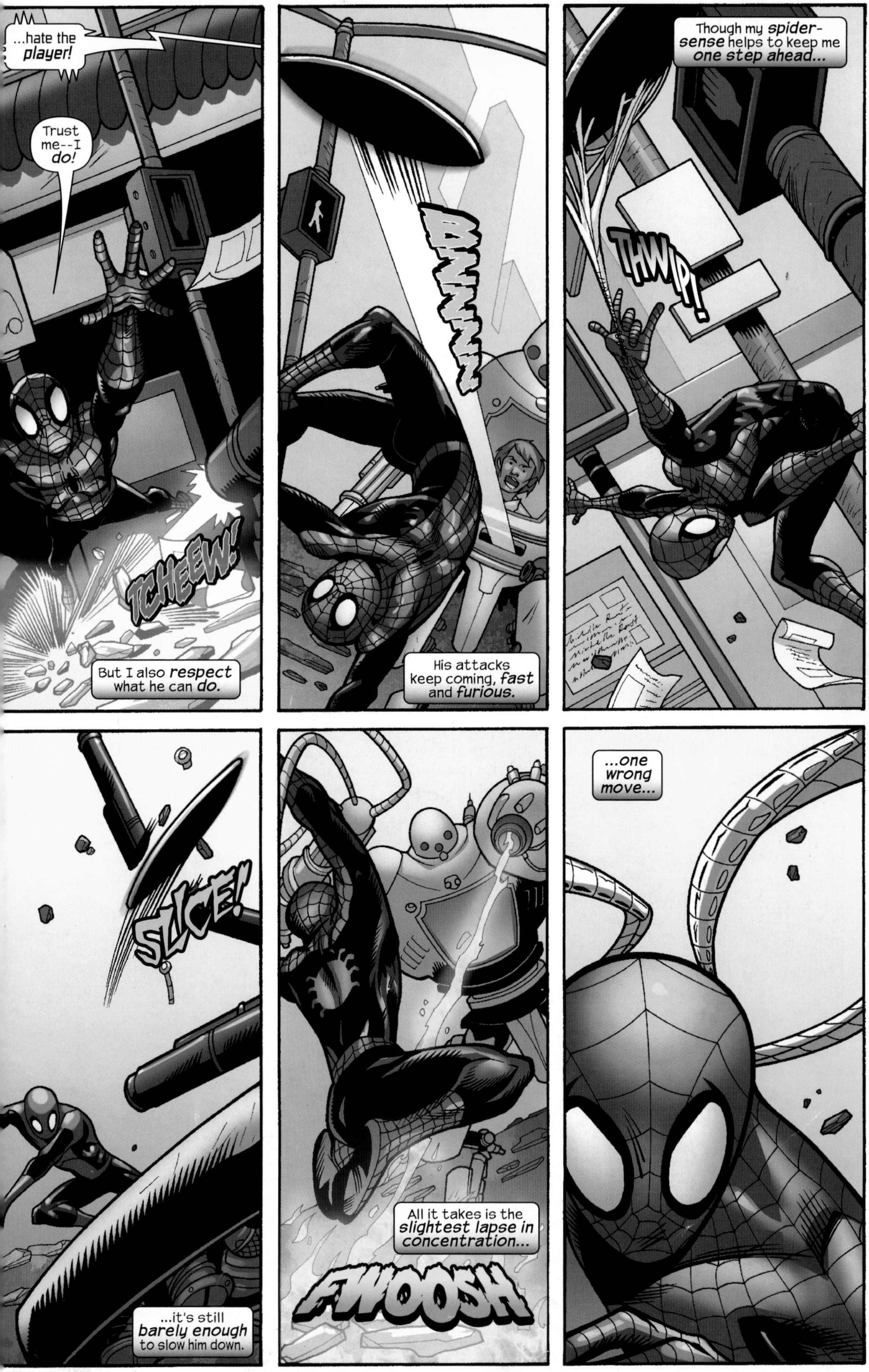

...hate the *player!*
Trust me--I *do!*
TCHEEW!
But I also *respect* what he can *do.*
BWNNN
His attacks keep coming, *fast* and *furious.*
Though my *spider-sense* helps to keep me *one step ahead...*
THWIP!
SLICE!
...it's still *barely enough* to slow him down.
All it takes is the *slightest lapse in concentration...*
FWOOSH
...one wrong move...

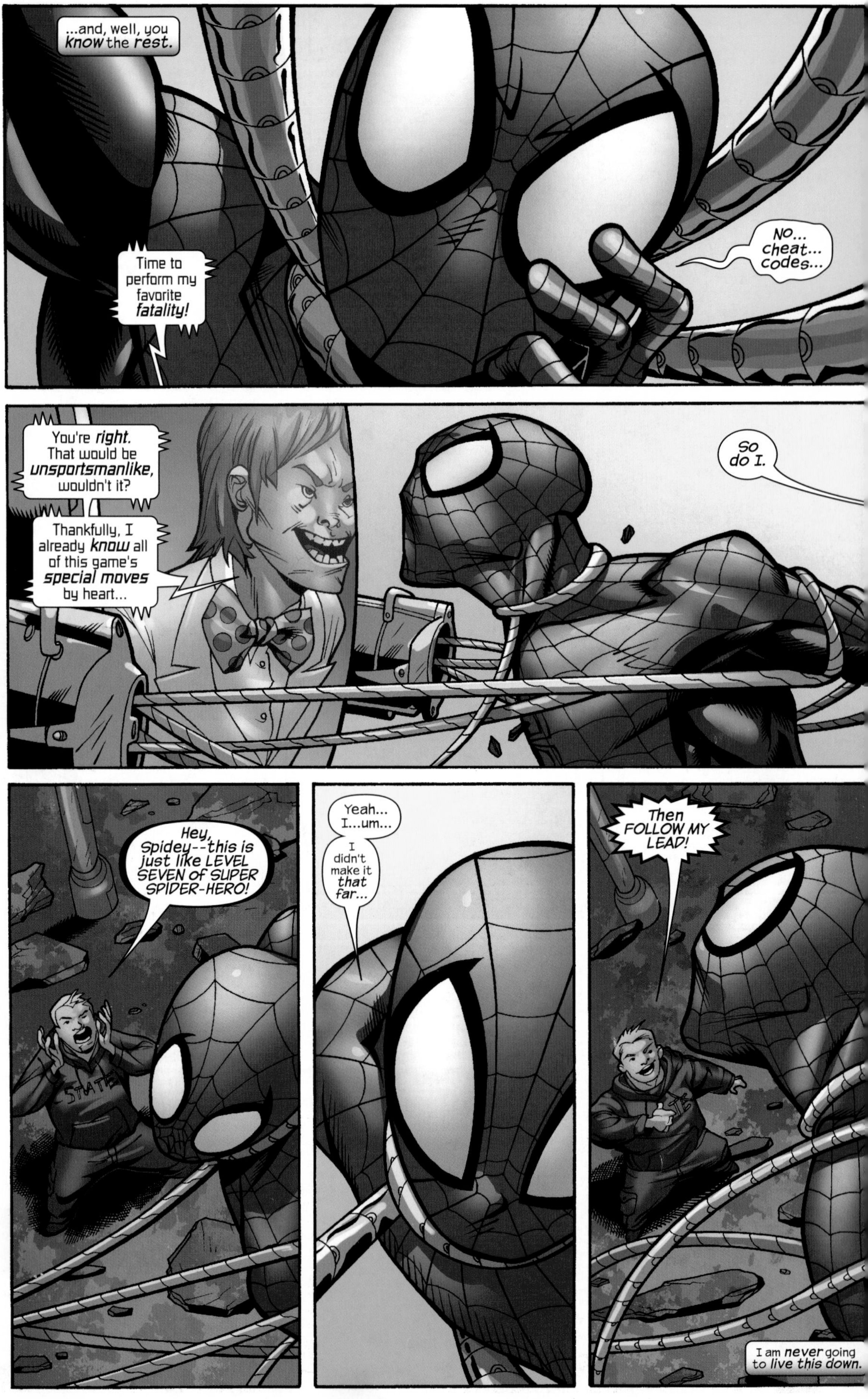
...and, well, you know the rest.
Time to perform my favorite fatality!
No... cheat... codes...
You're right. That would be unsportsmanlike, wouldn't it?
Thankfully, I already know all of this game's special moves by heart...
So do I.
Hey, Spidey--this is just like LEVEL SEVEN of SUPER SPIDER-HERO!
Yeah... I...um...
I didn't make it that far...
Then FOLLOW MY LEAD!
I am never going to live this down.

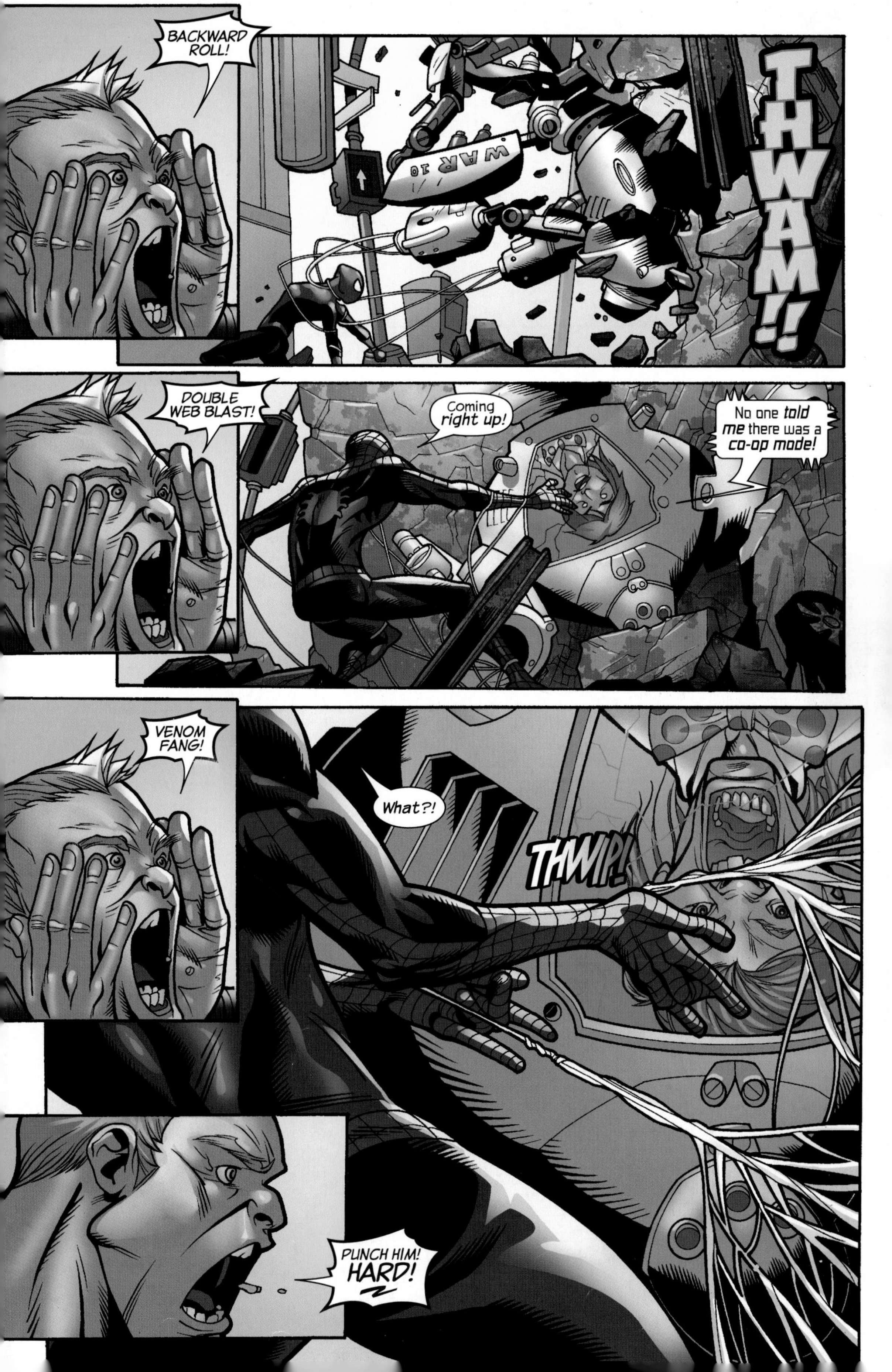

BACKWARD ROLL!
WAR 10
THWAM!!
DOUBLE WEB BLAST!
Coming right up!
No one told me there was a co-op mode!
VENOM FANG!
What?!
THWIP!
PUNCH HIM! HARD!

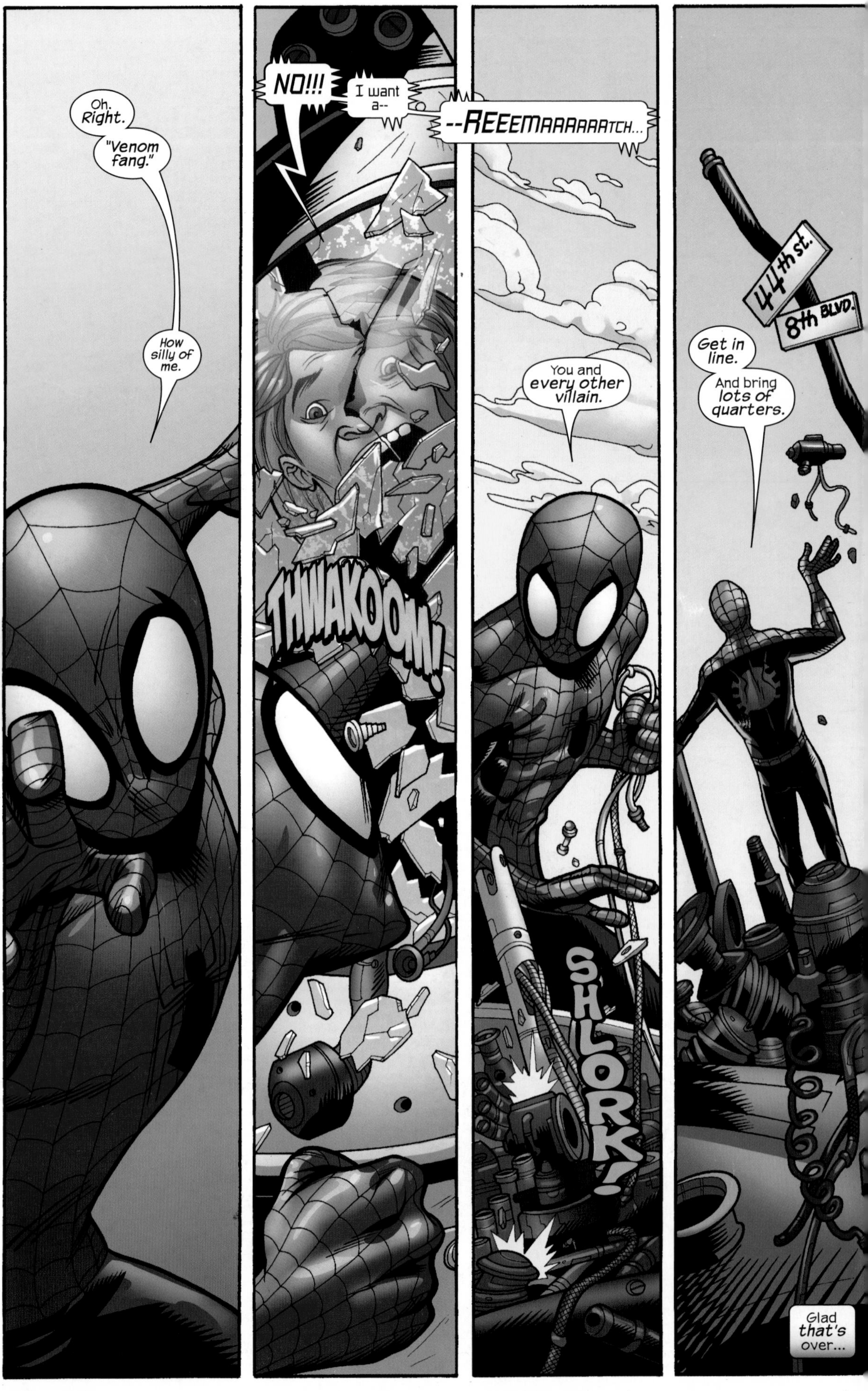
Oh. Right.
"Venom fang."
How silly of me.
NO!!!
I want a--
--REEEMAAAAAAATCH...
THWAKOOM!
You and every other villain.
SHLORK!
44th st.
8th BLVD.
Get in line.
And bring lots of quarters.
Glad that's over...

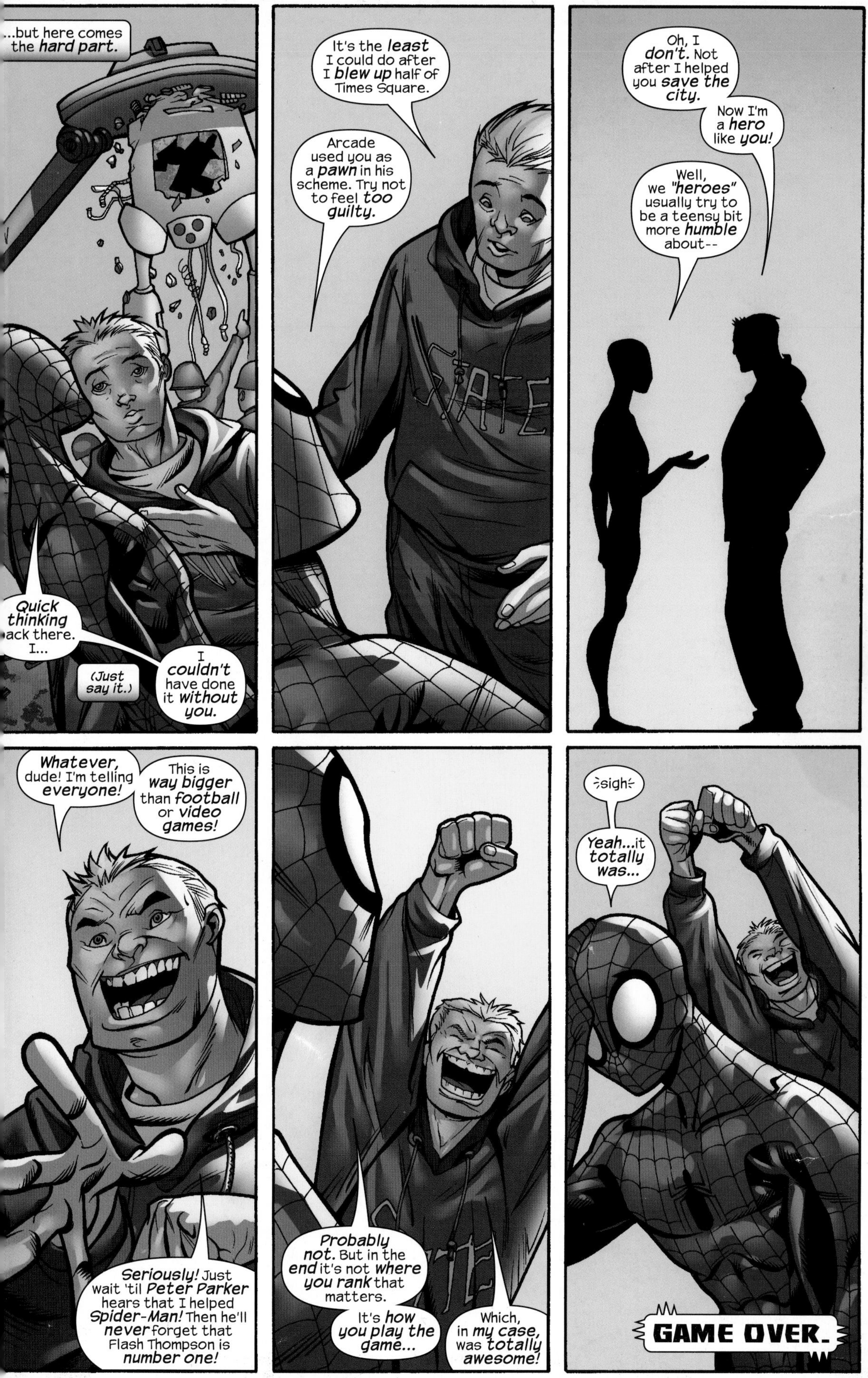
...but here comes the hard part.
Quick thinking ack there. I...
(Just say it.)
I couldn't have done it without you.
It's the least I could do after I blew up half of Times Square.
Arcade used you as a pawn in his scheme. Try not to feel too guilty.
Oh, I don't. Not after I helped you save the city.
Now I'm a hero like you!
Well, we "heroes" usually try to be a teensy bit more humble about--
Whatever, dude! I'm telling everyone!
This is way bigger than football or video games!
Seriously! Just wait 'til Peter Parker hears that I helped Spider-Man! Then he'll never forget that Flash Thompson is number one!
Probably not. But in the end it's not where you rank that matters.
It's how you play the game...
Which, in my case, was totally awesome!
sigh
Yeah...it totally was...
GAME OVER.

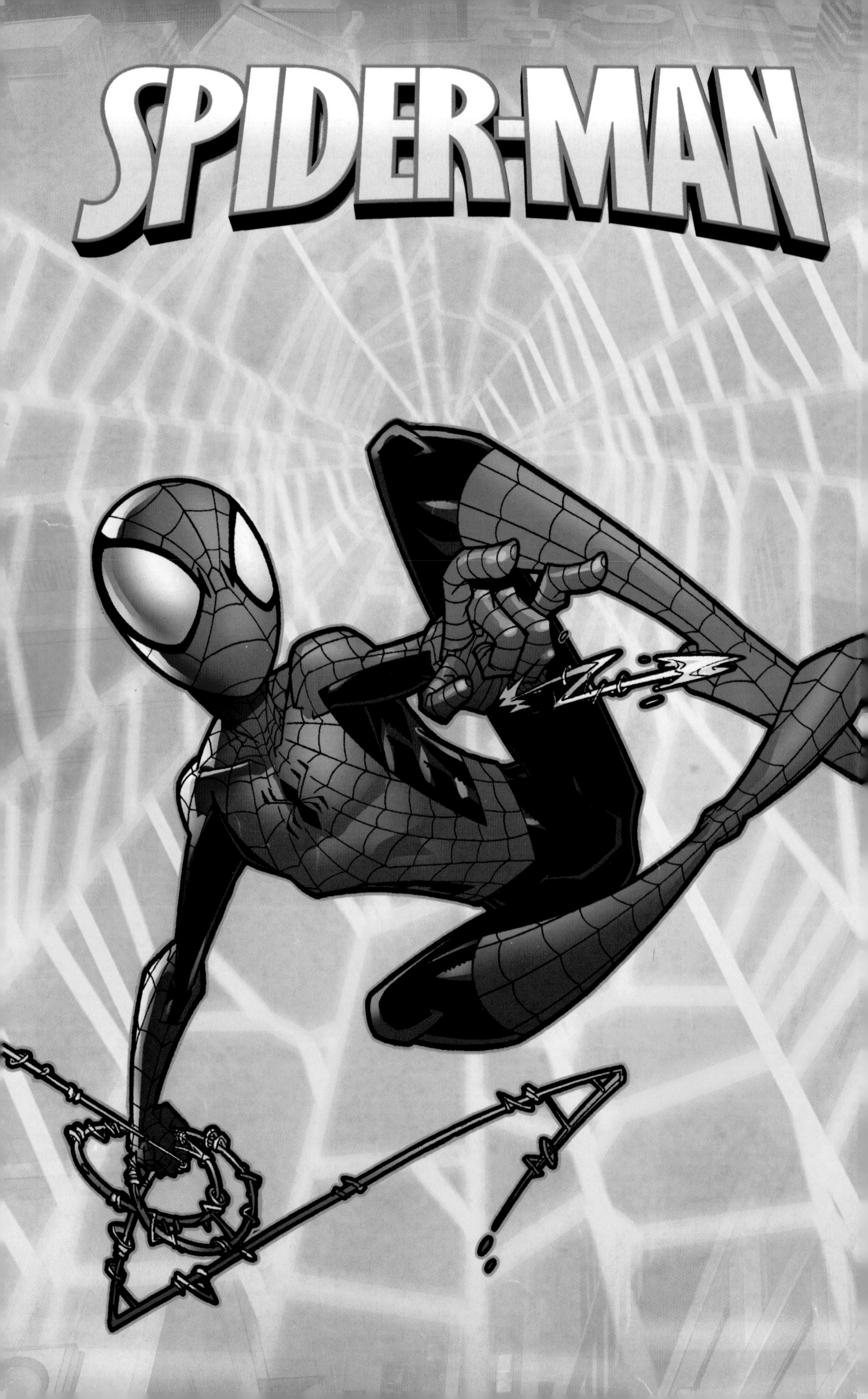
SPIDER-MAN